Betty the Yeti
PLAYS HIDE-AND-SEEK

by Mandy R Marx

illustrated by Antonella Fant

raintree

a Capstone company — publishers for children

Raintree is an imprint of Capstone Global Library Limited, a company incorporated in England and Wales having its registered office at 264 Banbury Road, Oxford, OX2 7DY – Registered company number: 6695582

www.raintree.co.uk
myorders@raintree.co.uk

Designed by Hilary Wacholz
Original illustrations © Capstone Global Library Limited 2024
Originated by Capstone Global Library Ltd

978 1 3982 5258 5

British Library Cataloguing in Publication Data
A full catalogue record for this book is available from the British Library.

Printed and bound in India.

CONTENTS

MEET BETTY AND HER FAMILY

Betty Yeti and her family moved from a cold mountain home to an apartment in the city. Mama Yeti, Betty and her twin brothers, Eddy and Freddy, are the only yetis in town. Getting used to a new place is hard. But it's especially hard when you're a yeti who isn't quite ready to stand out.

Mama

Eddy

Betty

Freddy

Chapter 1

BETTY LEARNS A NEW GAME

Betty Yeti and her family were at their local park. Betty's friends were there too. Everyone was enjoying the fresh spring air. Well, almost everyone.

"I'm bored," said George.

"Let's play hide-and-seek," said Elsie.

Cecilia nodded her head.

Betty didn't know that game. But it sounded fun. Sometimes she felt shy and wanted to hide!

"How do you play?" Betty asked.

"You all hide," said Cecilia. "And I won't look. After I count to twenty, I'll search for you."

Chapter 2

NOWHERE TO HIDE

"One, two, three," said Cecilia, covering her eyes.

Elsie ran behind a recycling bin. George squeezed under a slide.

Betty looked around her. She was too tall to stand behind a recycling bin. And she couldn't fit under the slide.

"Eighteen, nineteen . . ."

Cecilia had almost finished counting.

Betty ran behind a tree. It was taller than her. But was it wider? Betty tried to make herself tall and straight. It was no use.

"Twenty. Ready or not, here I come!" said Cecilia.

Betty heard her friend running towards her. "I found Betty!" she said.

Betty sighed as Cecilia
kept looking.

"Elsie, George, where
are you?" called Cecilia.

Betty couldn't believe she
didn't see them. But at last,
Cecilia found them both.

"Now I'm the seeker!" said Elsie. She started counting.

George got into a tube slide. Cecilia went under some steps.

Betty's heart raced.

Elsie counted even faster

than Cecilia did. In a panic,

Betty ran behind a lampost.

Elsie opened her eyes.

She burst out laughing.

"Betty!" she said.

"You have to at least *try*."

Betty tried to smile. But the truth was, she wasn't having any fun.

Chapter 3

ONE LAST SHOT

Next it was George's turn.

Elsie ran behind a bush.

Cecilia climbed a tree.

For a third time, Betty was stumped. The only place where she could hide was behind another yeti.

Luckily, Eddy was sitting down playing his video game. He didn't notice Betty crouch behind him. Betty was happy she'd found a hiding place.

"Nineteen, twenty," shouted George. "Ready or not, here I come!"

Just then, Eddy scored in his game. He jumped up and yelled, "YES!"

Betty was now in plain sight.

"I see Betty!" called George.

Betty covered her face with her hands.

"That's it," she said, "I'm done." And she ran off crying.

Cecilia walked towards Betty.

But Eddy put a hand on Cecilia's
shoulder.

"Let me talk to her," he said.

Chapter 4

BETTY'S STRENGTHS

"Sorry I messed up your hiding place, sis," Eddy said.

Betty gave him a little smile. "It's okay," she said. "I'm not very good at this game."

"You might not be good at hiding," Eddy said. "But what about seeking?"

Betty hadn't thought of that.
She could always spot her friends'
hiding places.

"Use your strengths," said
Eddy. "We yetis may be big,
but we're also tall."

That was it! Betty smiled.
"I know what my strength is
now," she said.

Betty went to find Cecilia.

"Could I be the seeker all the time?" Betty asked Cecilia.

"Probably not *all* the time," said Cecilia. "But you can have my turn now!"

Cecilia was a good friend.

Betty smiled and covered her eyes. "One, two, three . . ."

Betty's friends ran to find new hiding places. At last, Betty shouted, "Ready or not, here I come!"

Glossary

crouch   bend down at the knees

panic   sudden feeling of worry

recycling   process of using materials again instead of throwing them away

seek   look for something, or someone, that is hidden or lost

strength   strong quality

Talk about it

1. Betty had to learn how to play hide-and-seek. Have you ever learned a new game? Was it easy to learn? Did you like it?

2. If you were Betty, would you have found different places to hide? How would you have played the game differently?

3. Cecilia was kind to Betty at the end of the story. Can you think of a time when you were kind to a friend during a game?

Write about it

1. Cecilia explained the rules of hide-and-seek to Betty. Think of your favourite playground game. Write down instructions for playing the game. Make sure you include the rules of the game.

2. Eddy helped Betty think about her strengths. Think about something you are good at doing. Write about what makes it one of your strengths.

3. Betty asked Cecilia to change the game's rules at the end of the story. Think about how the rules could be different so that Betty could be the seeker more often. Write about how you would change the game.

About the author

Mandy R Marx is a writer and editor. She lives in a chilly town in Minnesota, USA, with her husband, daughter and a white, silky haired pup. She has a curious mind and stays on the lookout for yetis. In her spare time, Mandy enjoys singing, laughing with friends and family and walking her pup through what she suspects is a magical forest.

About the illustrator

María Antonella Fant is a visual designer, children's book illustrator and concept artist. Her illustrations reflect her childish, restless and curious personality, taking inspiration from animated cartoons and children's books from her childhood. María enjoys the way a child thinks, drawing like them and for them. María was born, and currently lives, in Argentina.